Kenny
and the
Blue Sky

by Richard Kopley

illustrated by Jane Ramsey

Eifrig Publishing LLC

Lemont　　Berlin

At Eifrig Publishing, our motto is our mission —
"Good for our kids, good for our Earth, and good for our communities."

We are passionate about helping kids develop into caring, creative, thoughtful individuals who possess positive self-images, celebrate differences, and practice inclusion. Our books promote social and environmental consciousness and empower children as they grow in their communities.
www.eifrigpublishing.com

For Nathanael and Claire
– R.K.

For my mother, Carole
– J. R.

Published by Eifrig Publishing,
PO Box 66, Lemont, PA 16851, USA
Knobelsdorffstr. 44, 14059 Berlin, Germany.

For information regarding permission, write to:
Rights and Permissions Department,
Eifrig Publishing,
PO Box 66, Lemont, PA 16851, USA.
permissions@eifrigpublishing.com, +1-888-340-6543

Library of Congress Cataloging-in-Publication Data

Kopley, Richard
Kenny and the Blue Sky/
by Richard Kopley, illustrated by Jane Ramsey
p. cm.

Paperback: ISBN 978-1-63233-012-3
Hard cover: ISBN 978-1-63233-013-0

[1. Imagination – Juvenile Fiction.]

I. Ramsey, Jane ill. II. Title

22 21 20 19 2018

5 4 3 2 1

Printed on acid-free paper. ∞

One fine spring morning, Kenny sat very still on his back steps and gazed up at the blue sky. Kenny loved the blue sky. The night sky was a little scary, and the gray sky was a little sad, but the blue sky was safe and cheerful and friendly. A few puffy white clouds drifted across the sky with ease. Kenny sat very still. He sat very still and wished he could be in the blue sky.

The clouds drifted on.

Kenny looked around the
backyard of the garden apartments.
At the playground, Miriam and Frances
were swinging, and Joey was climbing
up the steps of the big slide. Joey's little
brother was playing in the sandbox,
patting a mountain into shape.
And nearby, Kenny's parents
were sitting on beach chairs,
watching his sister Karen
in her playpen.

Kenny stood up to go play with his sister.
It was then that he glanced at the sky and noticed a slight
movement–barely a tremble, not quite a quiver.
He kept watching, thinking that something was about to happen.
And then Kenny saw what no one else saw:
slowly, ever so slowly,
the blue sky lowered itself.

Kenny stared. He was amazed and pleased.
He called to his parents, "Ma!" "Dad!" and pointed
at the blue sky as it slid through the upper air.
Kenny's parents looked up, looked at each other in
surprise, and looked up again. Kenny's sister Karen
held on to the bars of her playpen and looked up.
All the children stopped their playing
and looked up.

Slowly,
   slowly,
      slowly,

      the blue sky fell through the great space above.

Everyone waited.
The sky fell farther and farther.
After a long while, the sky fell to a place
just above Kenny's backyard.
As the blue overtook treetops and rooftops,
the wondering children began to
shout with excitement.

Miriam and Frances swung in and out of the blue. Joey stood proudly at the top of the big slide, covered by the blue. Joey's little brother made little jumps from the top of his mountain. And Kenny picked up his sister from her playpen and held her high. Her stubby fingers wiggled in the air.

Steadily the blue sky fell the last few feet.
Gently, quietly, it met the earth.
The children became still. No one uttered a sound.
Miriam and Frances and Joey and Joey's little brother
and Kenny and Kenny's sister and
Kenny's mom and dad were in the blue sky.

Kenny looked down.
The dandelions were green.

Kenny placed his sister in his mother's arms and breathed deeply. The blue tickled his nose at first, but he soon became used to its freshness and coolness. And he liked its faint scent of vanilla. Kenny looked through the vivid air. The children were exploring the blue, running, jumping, spinning. Their cries of delight seemed to come from a far distance. Kenny rushed through the sky with abandon.

Kenny whizzed and he whooped. He whirled and he tumbled.
He rolled and rolled, over and over, in the cool grass with the
other children. There was great gladness in the blue sky in Kenny's
backyard—gladness upon gladness.
Soon all the children lay on their backs, panting, laughing,
waiting for everything to stop turning.

They rested in the blue.
And everything was still.

Then they arose and felt a cool breeze against their skin.
And they beheld, with growing pleasure, splendid white clouds,
clouds of glory, drifting softly over the garden apartments.
The clouds eased lower and settled lightly in
the blue sky in Kenny's backyard.

Kenny and the others sped through
the blue to the nearest cloud.
They paused at the edge of the lofty vapor.
And they stepped in.

Inside was a gorgeous place.
Hanging above and all around were
veils of white mist and fantastic swirls
and shreds and wisps. Deep within lay
billows of thick whiteness.

And motion throughout was smooth and slow.

Kenny watched a white tuft turning gracefully.
With a short quick breath, he blew it to Joey,
who blew it to his little brother, who blew it to Miriam,
who blew it to Frances.
And so, the cloudful of children began to play.

First there was the blowing and pushing and fanning of
the white fluff and streamers. Next came a short game of tag
and another of hide-'n-go-seek. Then came the somersaulting
and leapfrogging and a very proper make-believe cloud-picnic.

After a while, a breeze came up, and the cloud drifted on. The children jumped up and ran with the cloud, trying to stay inside. But the breeze increased, and all the clouds rose in the blue sky in Kenny's backyard and grandly trailed away. The children watched with longing until the clouds could no longer be seen. Then they walked back slowly into the cool breeze.

And then the breeze blew into a wind, and the wind into powerful gusts. And the boys and the girls were whisked from the ground and tossed and tousled and rumpled about in the blue.

They were skyborne.

The children were astonished, then afraid, then thrilled.

In the midst of the blue above Kenny's backyard, they shrieked
and squealed and called to each other with joy.
Kenny joined in the clamor, loudly, happily, as he was bounced
and whiffled around with the others in the hilarious sky.
And he thought that this all seemed so strangely familiar—like
a long-forgotten dream or lullaby, only better.

And then the gusts diminished. And the wind became
a cradling breeze. And the children were wafted down, down
through the sky and set down in the blue backyard.
They wobbled, then steadied, in a hush.

They looked up to see where they'd been. Then they turned
to each other and burst into story—about the cloud
and the wind and the flight through the blue.

And as the story went on, Kenny glanced around the backyard
and noticed a slight stirring. He knew that the time had come.
The children quieted.
And then they all saw what they'd known all along they would see:
slowly, ever so slowly, the blue sky lifted itself.

Kenny watched as the blue arose from the earth
and climbed above shoulders and heads. And he stretched and
he jumped and he reached with the others—but the blue rose higher
yet. So the girls dashed back to the waiting swings and swung up
to the rising sky. And Joey dashed back to the top of the slide and
stood, once again, in the blue. But in moments the sky cleared the
swings and the slide and rose higher up, out of reach.

It ascended past rooftops and treetops, through the place
above Kenny's backyard, towards the great space above
and the far upper air.
Then Kenny called out, "Come back!"
And Miriam and Frances and Joey and Joey's little brother
called with Kenny, "Come back!"
"Come back! Come back! Come back!"

And the children waited.

They stared up in silence.
The sky rose a little, then stopped.
It hung in midair, unmoving.

"This is it," Kenny thought,
as he held his breath and watched,
watching for all time.

High above Kenny's backyard, the blue sky dipped—it dipped,
then suddenly plunged. The children gasped—then cheered.

The sky hurried closer and closer, filled the lower air,
and coolly pressed itself against the earth.

Kenny felt the cool rush and breathed the sweet vanilla.
And with great love he hugged the blue sky.

The sky held to the earth for a long moment.
The children ran through the blue, shouting jubilantly.
Then, the sky rose. It rose quickly, and the children became still.
No one uttered a sound. The sky slowed and hovered over Kenny's backyard–then it climbed, sure and fast, to its place in the upper air
.

Kenny followed its rapid ascent.

Then he looked down.
The dandelions were yellow.

The children called again, "Come back!" But this time the sky
did not return. The children grew restless; they began to look at
each other and shake their heads. There was some murmuring
and shrugging of shoulders. Finally, Joey's little brother
sighed, "I'm going home." And Joey and Miriam and
Frances agreed, "Me, too." Tired but smiling, the children
said their good-byes and wandered home. Kenny was alone.
A few puffy white clouds appeared and drifted
across the blue sky. Kenny lingered a moment
in the bright backyard, and then he, too,
wandered home.

Kenny's mom and dad had seen everything.
They didn't speak; their happiness was in their eyes.
As Kenny approached, his mother lightly touched his cheek.
And his father placed a hand upon his shoulder.
Kenny looked up at his parents and felt a little shy—
a little shy and somehow more himself
than he had ever been.
He held their hands tightly.

Then Kenny walked to the playpen,
where his sister Karen lay sleeping. He crouched down,
reached between the bars, and stroked her damp hair.
He wondered what she had seen and whether she
would remember. And he thought that one day
he would tell her the whole story.

Kenny stood up. His mother drew near, scooped up his
sleeping sister, and carried her inside for the rest of her nap.
His father followed to make lunch.

The screen door banged shut.

Kenny sat down on his back steps and gazed up at
the blue sky. The blue sky was safe and
cheerful and friendly. And it had a lived-in look.
Kenny spoke in his mind to the blue sky.
"Thank you," he said.
"Thank you, thank you, thank you. I will
always remember what happened
today." And he paused. He imagined
himself grown up and still remembering.

And he added, "If you ever come back—
I'll be waiting."